BITTER

AND

Sweet

DEMITRIA**LUNETTA**

An imprint of Enslow Publishing

WEST **44** BOOKS™

Please visit our website, www.west44books.com.
For a free color catalog of all our high-quality books,
call toll free 1-800-542-2595 or fax 1-877-542-2596.

Cataloging-in-Publication Data

Names: Lunetta, Demitria.
Title: Bitter and sweet / Demitria Lunetta.
Description: New York : West 44, 2021.
Identifiers: ISBN 9781538385234 (pbk.) | ISBN 9781538385241
  (library bound) | ISBN 9781538385258 (ebook)
Subjects: LCSH: Dating violence--Fiction. | Women--Violence
  against--Fiction. | Relationships--Fiction.
Classification: LCC PZ7.1.L868 Bi 2021 | DDC [F]--dc23
First Edition

Published in 2021 by
Enslow Publishing LLC
101 West 23rd Street, Suite #240
New York, NY 10011

Editor: Caitie McAneney
Designer: Seth Hughes

Photo Credits: cover (knife) Vladimirkarp/Shutterstock.com; cover
(ground) Abstractor/Shutterstock.com;

Printed in the United States of America

CPSIA compliance information: Batch #CW20W44: For further information contact
Enslow Publishing LLC, New York, New York at 1-800-542-2595.

AFTER

The cop is a woman. She doesn't look motherly or understanding. She looks mean. Mean and disgusted. Her suit is worn but clean.

They thought I would respond better to a woman. The truth is, I'll spill my guts to anyone who will listen. I feel the need to talk. It's like an itch I gotta scratch.

"We have to wait for your father to get here. You're a minor."

I shake my head. "My dad ain't gonna change nothin'. I killed the boy I loved most in the world."

She studies me, then leaves the interrogation room. I wonder how many people are watching me from the other side of that one-way mirror. Judging me. The way I talk. My torn jean shorts. The fading bruises on my arms. I sip my cola—the cheap stuff.

The cop returns with another, older woman. She has kind eyes and sensible brown shoes.

"Your father. He won't come. This is your appointed proxy guardian. Do you understand?"

I nod. Not surprised my daddy don't want nothing to do with me.

"You have to *say* you understand. For the tape." She pushes the table microphone toward me.

"I understand," I say. "This woman is here to make sure I don't say nothing stupid. But I don't need her. I'll tell you what happened if you want. I'll tell you all of it."

The women sit and wait for me to begin. Finally, I start.

"You have to understand," I say, my voice sounding desperate. I stop and take a deep breath. My shaking hand brings the soda can to my lips. I drink deeply, the sweet syrup taste helping to calm me.

I continue.

"Being in love with Tommy was like standing in line for a roller coaster. You're buzzing with excitement, but you're kind of fearful of what's coming. You also spend a lot of time hanging around for the payoff. And holy heck if it ain't worth the wait."

CHAPTER**ONE**

Three months ago

My stomach fills with eager dread as I push open the screen door to the rear of his house. Tommy's bedroom is back here. Even though it's three in the afternoon, he's probably just getting up. His school suspension hasn't fazed him at all.

Tommy says school ain't worth the time. There are plenty of ignorant people walking around with a high school diploma. School has always been hard for me, so I kinda agree with him on that.

"Tommy?" I call into the darkened house. I walk into the kitchen. My wet sneakers squeak on the floor. Then I go through to the living room. It rained during school and everything outside is covered in a thick slimy gloss. It shimmers in the afternoon heat.

I pause at his door. I hope he's not asleep. He won't like it if I wake him up. He'll be real mad. I take a step back. I'm about to retreat when I see him. A boy about Tommy's height but with dark brown hair instead of blond. "You ain't Tommy," I say stupidly.

"No... I'm not." He reaches over and switches on the living room light. It doesn't do much to brighten the house. Everything is old and worn and falling apart. Tommy doesn't come from money. Not that I do or anything.

For the first time I notice that the boy holds a knife in his hand. My stomach dips with fear.

CHAPTER**TWO**

I backpedal into the kitchen. Ready to bolt for the door. My wet sneakers slip on the smooth floor. I catch myself just before I trip.

The boy takes in my panic and hurriedly flicks his hand. The knife folds up neatly. "Sorry about the knife... I play with it when I'm bored," he explains. He places it in the pocket of his faded jeans. "I'm Loew... Tommy's cousin."

I relax slightly, let out a little laugh. "Shoot, you scared me half to death." I wipe my clammy hands on the back of my jean shorts. "I ain't never seen a knife like that."

"It's a butterfly knife. It's not really legal to carry it around," he says with a kind of shrug. I laugh a little. If there's one thing I expect from any cousin of Tommy's, it's to not worry about things being legal.

"Tommy said you were coming down for a visit...

where from again?"

"Georgia." He walks through to join me in the kitchen. He heads straight to the cabinet. Pulling out two glasses, he pours lemonade from a pitcher set out on the kitchen table. He offers me a glass and I step forward to take it, uncertain. Tommy doesn't like me talking to other boys. But his cousin should be okay... shouldn't he?

"I'm Sweetie... did Tommy say anything 'bout me?"

Loew's brow creases and he looks away. He says, "Oh yeah. Tommy told me all about you." The lie cuts through me. Tommy doesn't like to talk about things like emotions or relationships. He says we should just be what we are. But I know he loves me.

Loew chugs down his lemonade and pours himself another glass. "Sweetie... that's an interesting name."

"Loew ain't exactly common," I spit back.

"No... it isn't." He lifts his shirt to wipe his face. The action shows off a lean, well-muscled torso. The cloth comes away wet, drenched in sweat. "I don't know how you do it. It's so hot down here... October is supposed to be cool."

"Not in Florida it ain't," I tell him. I let out an uncomfortable giggle.

"And I thought Florida was all sandy beaches and Cuban restaurants."

I smile and take a sip of my lemonade. It's the pink

powdered kind that my brothers like. Too sickly sweet. "This ain't Miami," I tell him. "You won't find any beach bunnies around here. Just farmers and a buncha good ol' boy losers."

For some reason he finds this very funny. He almost chokes on his lemonade. Pink juice dribbles down his chin and onto the floor as he sputters. I laugh as I grab a kitchen towel. I help him clean up the mess.

"What's this now?" someone behind me asks.

That voice makes me feel like running. My brain can't decide if it should be away or toward.

CHAPTER**THREE**

I turn to find Tommy. He's watching us with a sour look. His shirt's off. His muscles tense. He runs his hand through his sandy blond hair.

"I just... I brought your homework like I said I would. Hey, I didn't know your cousin was here already." My eyes don't leave Tommy.

His face darkens. "You met Low-down? What do you make of him?"

"He's..." I don't know what Tommy wants me to say. "He sure does like lemonade."

Tommy gives a half-smile. He stares at me. I can tell he's thinking about what to do next. "You got my schoolwork?" he asks softly. I nod. "Then bring it." He turns and disappears into his room. I stand to follow.

"It was nice to meet you," Loew calls after me. I kind of grunt back. I can't manage anything more. I'm under Tommy's spell.

His room is darker than even the rest of the house. I close the door behind me. Let my backpack slide to the floor. This is it. Emotion burns like acid through my veins. Either way it goes, it's time to ride the roller coaster.

He turns to me and reaches for my face. I can't help but flinch. But his touch is gentle. I take in his scent, sun and cigarettes. He strokes my cheek. He leans down to whisper in my ear. "Sweetie."

And just like that, I melt. It's going to be one of the good days.

CHAPTER**FOUR**

I hate showering at home. The lock doesn't work. My brother's dirty dog friends take that as an invitation. They're always barging in "accidentally" to get a good eyeful. The days when I see Tommy, though, I have to shower at home or hear about it from Daddy.

Daddy may be too drunk most nights to know what day of the week it is, but he's got a nose like a bloodhound. If he thinks I smell like a boy, I won't hear the end of it.

I'm glad I took the time to drag a chair into the bathroom and jam it under the door handle because I'm not in the shower 30 seconds when someone is trying to push it open. I ignore the racket and take my sweet time. When I'm finished, I wrap myself in a towel, check to make sure the hallway's clear, and make my way to my room. Closing the door, I smile when I think that maybe Tommy texted. I search for my phone on my bed but can't find it.

I hear my door creak open behind me and my father looms in the doorway. I pull my towel up, my pink skin burning. Why hadn't I brought my clothes in the bathroom with me? I'm so stupid.

"You looking for this?" he asks, holding up my phone.

I nod and he tosses it at me. I grab for it, almost dropping my towel. "Were you checking up on me?" I ask. I always delete messages as soon as I read them, but if Tommy sent something while I was in the shower, I'm in for a beating for sure.

He looks me over now. "You're a good girl, Sweetie, but... you're growing up. You're looking more and more like your mama every day." My brothers both have my dad's light brown hair, but I got my mama's auburn color. I also got her figure, long legs and not much on top.

My Daddy looks me up and down. "Just because you look like her, don't mean I want you acting like her." My mama ran off when I was little. It sent Daddy to drinking. Sometimes he calls me her name when he's real drunk.

"I won't, Daddy... I gotta get dressed now. Okay?"

He gives me a hard look over. "Sure, Sweetie. Then come down for dinner. I made fried chicken."

Daddy's chicken is always tough and greasy, but I

say, "That sounds great." Even with his drinking, he still has a job. He still makes dinner and still tries to provide for me and my brothers. Trying... it's more than a lot of the other kids' dads do.

He shuts the door. I lock it after him, then sit on my bed in my wet towel and stare at my phone. I'm glad Tommy didn't text, but I'm also disappointed. That boy drives me crazy, but I can't imagine living without him.

CHAPTER**FIVE**

When I walk into Tommy's room the next day, I already know that it's going to be a bad time. There is nothing gentle in his touch. Even his smell is off, sharper, meaner. I know that no matter what I say, it will set him off. I back toward the door.

"Where you think you going?" he asks.

"I just gotta get home," I say.

"You too good to stick around? You think I'm a loser?"

"No, Tommy. God, no..."

He reaches out and slaps my face so suddenly I barely have time to register what's happened. If it weren't for the fresh burn on my cheek, I would think I'd dreamed it.

Then he's on me. He grabs my hair, pulling my face to his. When he's like this, it's best not to fight, to just go limp, so I let myself fall onto his bed and think of all the good times. I must be whimpering because he holds his hand over my mouth and pushes hard on my face. I close my eyes. I don't like seeing him like that.

After, I just lay there. Unsure if it's safe to get dressed and leave. I know it's all right when he lights a cigarette and asks, "You'll be by tomorrow?"

"'Course I will." I pull on my clothes and grab my bag. I stop at the door. Without turning around, I say, "I love you, Tommy."

"I love you too, Sweetie. You're the only girl for me."

"Do you think I can use your shower?" I ask, still facing the door.

"Sure, just don't be here after five. I don't want my mom seeing you and asking questions about us."

I nod. His mom works the day shift at the tire factory. Tommy likes to keep his private life private.

I leave the room, shutting the door behind me. I don't think there'll be a mark on my face. I don't bruise easily.

I place my hand on my cheek, cooling the burning skin.

There's a strange noise coming from the kitchen and I turn to find Loew sitting at the table, folding and unfolding his knife. His hand moves so quickly, I can barely see the blade. He looks up at me and I know he heard it all. Tommy's rage. Loew's face is blank though.

"I... Tommy said I could take a shower."

He shrugs. I head to the bathroom, locking the door behind me. I turn the shower on full blast. Crouching down, I rest my face on my knees. I try to stop the tears, but soon I begin to sob.

I can't help it. Sometimes my sadness washes over me like a river. It's all I can do to keep my head above the water. I don't want to drown in my feelings so I push them down, down, down, so far they're nothing but dark rocks on the riverbed. In my mind, I picture them as stepping stones. I use them to get myself out of the flood of misery.

Letting the last bit of sadness drip off of me, I take a deep breath and stand. I know I shouldn't let the way Tommy acts get me down. He's not always hurtful, just sometimes.

After I collect myself, I shower quickly, hoping to avoid Loew as I leave. But he's waiting for me on the back porch.

"You okay, Sweetie?" His dark eyes shine.

"Fine," I say quickly. "See you tomorrow."

I run from him because it's easier than explaining. Tommy is mine and all the good outweighs all the bad. I love him, and loving Tommy means that you never know if you're going to get a kiss or a slap.

CHAPTER**SIX**

In American History class the next day, that piece of bleach-blonde-white-trash Krissy Dawson sits behind me and starts running her mouth about Tommy.

"I heard he has a meth lab in his basement. He got busted and sent to prison."

I turn around and glare at her and her friends. She smiles at me with her pink-glossed lips and smacks her gum. "Sorry, Sweetie. Do you need something?"

I turn back, and silently fume. It's not like I can correct her. Then she'd wonder why I was defending Tommy Hicks.

From the desk next to Krissy's, Jeanie Riley says loudly, "I wish people wouldn't talk about things they know nothing about." She pointedly turns to Krissy. "Oh, but then you wouldn't ever say anything."

Someone meows from behind Jeanie, and Krissy puckers her lips, holding in her comeback. I flash

Jeanie a grateful smile, but she doesn't return it. Jeanie and I have been friends since preschool... well, had been friends. Jeanie is one of the few people who knows about Tommy and me. Even though she thinks Tommy ruined our friendship, Jeanie's kept our relationship a secret. She knows my dad would kill me if he found out I had a boyfriend.

I didn't mean to stop being friends with Jeanie, but Tommy hates her... I'm not quite sure why. Maybe because she lets people know what she thinks. Like she just did with Krissy. I would never speak to anyone like that. Even to defend Tommy.

Yes, he'd been suspended and yes it was for having meth in his locker, but he ain't got no lab. His lock was broken too, so they couldn't even prove it was his. All he got was a two-week suspension. I know people think Tommy is rough, but they don't know him. They don't know how sweet he can be.

During class, I start to deflate. There's a quiz and I don't know any of the answers. I didn't study. Krissy popping her gum behind my head is giving me a headache.

By the time the bell rings, I'm 'bout ready to jump out of my skin. Jeanie catches me in the hall and walks with me to my locker. "So... still with Tommy?"

"Yeah." When I hooked up with Tommy, I stopped talking to all my old friends, not just Jeanie. It just sorta happened. I don't even know how. "I was going to ditch out of study hall to go see him," I admit.

She nods and opens her mouth to say something. Then she thinks better of it. She starts again, "Sweetie, I know I've been cold to you, but... I miss you."

"We got a buncha classes together." I know that ain't what she means.

"Sure, but there's always people around and we can't really talk. Maybe this weekend you can come over."

I don't need to ask what she wants to talk about. Jeanie wants to tell me again what she thinks of Tommy. I really don't need to hear it. "I can't this weekend. I got work and then my dad wants me home." Her face falls. "Maybe next weekend," I offer. I'm not good at saying no.

"Okay, I guess." Her face is pinched.

"See ya," I slam my locker shut and make a run for the door before the bell rings. A lot of seniors ditch last period study hall and no one really stops them. I blend in with them and make my way to my truck.

As I drive, I wonder what Jeanie will say that is different than last time. Tommy's no good for me. He likes trouble too much. He's white trash and does too many drugs. I pull into Tommy's driveway with a sigh. I wish Jeanie was wrong, but she ain't. Tommy's all those things. But he's also street-smart and funny and so handsome it makes me flush just thinking about him.

I drive a little faster.

His love is my drug.

CHAPTER**SEVEN**

At Tommy's house, I head inside. Loew is in the kitchen, having himself a big glass of lemonade. He looks up at me and then at the clock. "Ain't you supposed to be in school?"

I don't like his tone, like he's disappointed in me. Like he has any right.

"Ain't you got anywhere else to be, like *ever*?" I shoot back, surprising myself.

I expect him to get mad—Tommy sure would have—but he just chuckles. I realize he wasn't trying to be mean to me.

"That's how it must look to you... like I'm always here."

He takes out his knife absently and flicks it open. He twists his hand and closes it. I'm actually getting used to the idea of Loew with a knife, like it's a part of him.

"Well, ain't ya?" I smile. "Shouldn't *you* be in school?"

"Nah...I'm done with school. Got out last year. My aunt got me a job down at the tire factory. Graveyard shift. I'm just waking up now."

"So you're on Tommy's schedule," I tease. "Rise and shine at two in the afternoon."

"Yeah. I think he really likes being suspended. I don't think he'll want to go back."

I don't want to think about school without Tommy being there. It's only been a week and it's killing me. I always try to sit behind him in class so I can stare at him without people thinking I'm a freak. I sigh and focus on Loew.

"So you're having lemonade for breakfast?"

He shrugs. "I was going to make some frozen pizza."

"Gross." I drop my bag on the floor and walk over to the fridge. There's not much, but there's the basics: eggs, bacon, butter. I start pulling out food. "I'm gonna cook you a proper breakfast."

"You don't have to do that," he tells me, tilting his head. Despite his protests, his eyes shine, like I just told him he's won the lottery.

I look through the cabinets. "Fine, I'll make myself some breakfast and you can watch me eat." I find a pan and fry up the bacon and eggs. I finish it all up with some buttered toast. Since Mama left, it was: learn to cook, eat Daddy's horrible food, or starve.

I plate up the food and place it in front of Loew. He does this funny deep breath thing, like it's the best thing he's ever smelled. When he takes a bite, his face breaks out into a smile.

"Better than frozen pizza?" I ask.

"Much better," he tells me, his mouth full. He takes a sip of lemonade.

"Next time, I'll make you some real lemonade," I tell him. "My mama used to make the best."

He puts his cup down. "Used to?" he asks. "Did she...?"

"Run off to Texas with some lowlife? Yep, she sure did." I laugh a little to show him it doesn't hurt, even though it does.

"Sweetie, Low-down, what's all this?" Tommy asks, stepping into the kitchen.

He's wearing nothing but his shorts and I can't help but look him up and down. I don't know how he stays so fit when he doesn't do a lick of work. Even with dabbling in meth, he's still the best-looking boy I've ever laid eyes on. Jeanie says it's early yet and in two years Tommy's going to look like he's 40 years old. Don't get her started on what she thinks Tommy's teeth will look like then.

I wonder how Loew and I seem to Tommy, sitting

here like friends or something. I must look real scared because Loew's face goes blank. He nods at Tommy.

"Sweetie wanted to make you breakfast. It smelled so good I helped myself."

Tommy scratches his stomach and grabs two beers from the fridge. He comes to sit at the table and places one of the beers in front of me. I don't even bother opening it. I can't stand the smell. It reminds me of my dad late at night. I push my plate in front of him, pleased he looks happy.

Tommy takes a big bite and a swig of beer and gives a satisfied grunt. He looks at me and winks. "Sweetie, you should skip school tomorrow. We'll spend the day together."

It's not really a question, so I don't have to answer. I can't help but grin. I hear a sigh come from Loew's direction. I catch him staring daggers at Tommy. It's just a flash of something unpleasant and his face goes back to normal. He pushes his plate away and stands.

"Thanks for breakfast, Sweetie."

I don't dare smile at him with Tommy there. I just shrug.

Tommy takes his last bite, then focuses on me. "Now what are we going to get up to?" he asks, reaching over and pulling me onto his lap. He tickles my neck with his mouth, making me giggle.

By the time we leave the kitchen, I'm breathless

and my skin feels all tingly. He can keep his meth. Tommy's the only thing I need to feel good.

CHAPTER**EIGHT**

I wish I could hold on to those happy feelings all night, but by the time dinner rolls around, my brothers are really testing my patience. Daddy brought home burgers and milkshakes and said we could eat in front of the TV. I got stuck sitting on the couch, which is lumpy and smells like boy funk. My 11-year-old brother Jimmy sits right next to me. He's practically on my lap. His hand brushes against my leg. It makes my skin crawl. I scoot over farther.

"Why are you always so close to me, Jimmy?" I ask.

"Leave him alone," Matt says. He shoves fries into his greasy face.

"He's always trying to touch me. It ain't right," I huff.

It's annoying. Jimmy used to be real nice too. He'd let me have the best seat and even bring me a soda if he was getting one from the kitchen. Then Matt started getting on his case and calling him names. Like being nice is a weakness. Like treating me like a person was bad. Now Jimmy is a mini-Matt. All he talks about is sports, girls' bodies, and sometimes cars.

"He's just curious. It's natural," Daddy says from the other side of the couch.

"Yeah, maybe if you didn't go around wearing those shorts with your butt practically hanging out..." Matt says. I don't let him finish. Living in this house is like living in a different century. I stand up and bring my food to my room. I eat on my bed while watching movies on my really old laptop.

Sometimes I wonder if it would be different if Mama were still around. I wouldn't be the only girl in the house. Maybe Matt and Jimmy would learn to treat me like a human. I usually don't let it bother me. They're just ignorant. But for some reason tonight I have a low tolerance for my family.

I sip my milkshake and frown. It's vanilla even though I like chocolate. Daddy never remembers. He gets vanilla because the boys like it. I sigh. Daddy can't see what a loser Matt is. In his eyes, that boy walks on water.

My daddy opens my door, not bothering to knock as usual. I jump a little but then relax. I can see he's not too drunk and he doesn't look mad or anything.

"Sweetie," he starts, then pauses like he doesn't

know what to say. "You know I'm trying to do my best. I do fine with Matt and Jimmy, but you being a girl and all..." He just stands there looking at me like I'm a different species.

"It's okay, Daddy," I say.

"I'll try to make sure the boys don't give you too much of a hard time," he tells me with a smile. For a moment, I remember how when I was a little girl he used to hug me and tell me I was special. I think we were happy then... before Mama left and ruined everything.

"Thanks, Daddy," I say with a smile. He really does try. He shuts the door. I'm about to restart the movie when my phone vibrates.

I check it. There's a message from Tommy asking what I'm up to. I'm about to text back about my annoying family, but I decide against it. Tommy doesn't want to hear about my problems. Instead I type:

Wish you were here with me.

Tommy doesn't always text back right away, but it is seconds before my phone vibrates again. I grin and try to think what flirty things Tommy would like me to say. It's nice to think he's as hooked as I am.

CHAPTER**NINE**

I leave the next morning at the same time I do every day. Instead of heading to school, I drive to Tommy's. My truck is a zillion years old. It was my Mama's. Daddy can't stand that it's still around, but I claimed it before he could think to sell it. No one would want to buy it anyway. By rights, Matt should have gotten it, but he was too embarrassed to drive such a piece of junk. At least I never have to drive him anywhere. He mostly relies on his loser friends for rides to school.

I pull up behind Tommy's house and cut the engine. His mom's shift starts at seven, so she's long gone. I check my makeup in the cracked side mirror and head up to the house.

Loew's sitting on the back porch, still wearing his blue factory jumpsuit. "Hey, Sweetie."

"Hey," I say. I try to breeze past him. I can't wait to see Tommy. Loew stands and steps in my way.

"He ain't here. I just checked. He wasn't home when I left for work last night either."

"But..." I close my eyes, disappointment washing over me. "He said..."

"I know. I was there. Tommy is..." He stops himself. "Hey look, you made me breakfast yesterday. It's only fair I buy you breakfast today. I'm not Tommy, but you're already ditching. We might as well do something, right?"

I think about it for a moment. Tommy wouldn't like it one bit. But Tommy isn't here. It serves him right, me eating breakfast with another boy. "Yeah, okay. You need to change?"

"Nah." He unbuttons the top part of the jumpsuit, revealing a white cotton shirt. "Unless you're embarrassed to be seen with me in my overalls."

I snort. "Once when I was little, my dad dropped me off at Girl Scouts wearing nothing but his tightywhities and a baseball cap. I can deal with a jumpsuit."

He raises his eyebrows. "Girl Scouts?"

"It's kind of a requirement around here. That and Sunday school." Although to be honest, once my Mama left, I stopped going to both. I motion over my shoulder at my truck. "I gotta warn you that there's no AC."

"Well, it's better than no car at all... which is what I have." He wriggles out of the top of his jumpsuit and lets it hang down around his legs.

We get in my truck and head over to the McDonald's. I glance over at him. He's cute. His dark features make him look mysterious. I catch sight of his ID badge hanging around his neck. "Why do you have your aunt's last name... isn't Hicks her married name?"

He looks over at me, a half smile on his lips. "It's a long story," he says. Taking off the badge, he places it in his pocket.

I can't help but peek at him again. I can't help but want to know more about him.

CHAPTER**TEN**

When we get to McDonald's, I order a chocolate milkshake and take it to the area outside. I sit on a table, stretching my legs and enjoying the morning sun. Loew gets a bunch of breakfast stuff and dumps it next to me.

"Are you sure all you want is a chocolate milkshake?" he asks.

"Yep," I say. Then laugh. "I'm happy with this. My daddy always gets us vanilla because that's what my brothers like."

"Can't he just order one different for you?" He shoves an entire egg and biscuit sandwich into his mouth.

"No, it ain't that. I just feel bad reminding him what I like." I take a long sip. It's been awhile since I sat with a friend and talked about my life. Loew nods, waiting for me to continue. "And I don't want to cause a fuss over a stupid milkshake. He already wants me home most of the time. As long as I keep my legs crossed and my mouth shut, I get to keep what little freedom I have."

"So he doesn't know about Tommy?"

I nearly choke on my milkshake. "Oh, heck no," I spit out. "He would beat my butt black and blue if he knew about Tommy."

I think Loew is staring at my legs. It's not strange. I'm used to boys looking me up and down. It's just how boys are, I guess. I'm surprised when I glance over. Loew's focused on my feet of all things.

"Does he hit you much?"

I don't know if he means my daddy or Tommy.

"My dad?" I guess. "No, not a lot. Hardly at all really. Sometimes I think..."

I barely know Loew and I can feel myself crossing a line, but I never get to talk about myself. Now that I've started, it's hard to stop. Jeanie was a great friend, but even before Tommy she always had to put in her two cents. She always had to tell me what she thought and what I should do. Loew asks questions like he actually wants to hear what I have to say.

I swallow a sip of milkshake and go on. "Part of it, I think, is that I remind my daddy too much of my mama. He don't like to think about me 'cause then he thinks of her. When he's had a lot to drink, he looks at me like I *am* her. Like I just came back to be with him. Sometimes, if I don't catch how far gone he is, he grabs me. He tries to kiss me 'cause he really thinks I'm her."

I take a deep breath and force my sadness down to that place where I don't have to deal with it. "I push him off, though, tell him I'm getting him another beer, and then lock myself in my room. He's real easy to distract when he's drunk like that... and he doesn't remember nothing the next morning."

I've never even told Jeanie about this. It feels good to get it off my chest.

Loew examines me. I expect his face to be full of pity but instead he looks like he understands. He rubs the black stubble on his chin, his eyes dark.

I'm done with all my whining and feeling sorry for myself. Loew is looking real sad. I hop down off the table and sit next to him. I try to change the subject.

"What's up with you and that knife anyway?"

He looks down at it. "Oh, it's just something that calms me." He places the closed knife in front of me. "Try it."

I reach out, the metal warm from his grip. I try to flick it open but only manage to throw it across the table. I make an *eep* noise and laugh at my own clumsiness.

Loew reaches across and hands it back to me. "Don't worry, you just need to practice. Keep it."

"Really?" I ask. "You seem to love this thing."

"Nah, it's just a way to deal with stress. You need it more than I do."

I push it back to him, but then change my mind and clutch it to my chest. "Thank you, Loew. That's real nice of you."

"It's nothing, Sweetie... is that actually your name?"

"No," I shrug. "It's just what everyone calls me."

He looks at me, waiting. "Are you going to tell me what your name really is?"

"Maybe one day." I flash him a half smile. He grins back.

My phone buzzes in my pocket. It's a text from Tommy asking where the heck I am. It's like he could sense that I was flirting with another boy.

"I gotta go... it's Tommy." My smile disappears. "I don't know what he would think if we drove up together..." I look away from him, guilty. I know it ain't right to ditch Loew but I don't feel like getting into a fight with Tommy today.

"It's fine," he says. His voice is strained like it's anything but fine. "I'll walk back."

"You sure?" I ask, getting to my feet. I give him a friendly nudge with my shoulder. "Thanks for breakfast and the talk... but maybe, let's not tell Tommy about this."

"I won't." This time he just looks annoyed.

I go to my car and try not to look back at Loew. I can't help it as I drive away. He still sits at the table, his head in his hands. He looks real beat down.

I think about my life and all the things I just admitted to him. I feel myself begin to tear up. By the time I get to Tommy's, I have to sit in the driveway for five minutes before I'm ready to go inside.

I step out of the car and put a smile on my face as bright as the Florida sunshine.

CHAPTER**ELEVEN**

The weekends suck because I can't get away to see Tommy. I work at the Dairy Queen part-time to pay for gas. My daddy's home the whole time, drinking. He knows my schedule by heart. He wants me home half an hour after my shift ends, no exceptions. It kills me not to be over at Tommy's for a whole two days. On Monday, I skip seventh period again.

When I get to his house, Tommy's still asleep. I should have known. Loew's there, though. I have another talk with him, this time about where he's from up in Georgia, and how he was sorry to leave. He said he had to, though. When I ask why, he changes the subject. After that we talk about music. We both love oldies, though I wouldn't admit that to Tommy. He thinks I love EDM.

I skip again Tuesday, because let's be honest, study hall is a joke. Wednesday and Thursday, I do the same.

By Friday, I have to come clean with myself: I'm going to Tommy's early just so I can talk with Loew. I don't want to admit it, but I like him. I like being around him. I like talking to him about nothing. I like playing with the knife he gave me. I'm getting better at flicking it open.

If being with Tommy is like waiting for a roller coaster, being with Loew is like sitting in a restaurant waiting for a chocolate sundae. There's no dread, just eagerness, and the payoff is always sweet. But then I always feel sick afterward. Like I've done something bad. Even though I haven't done nothin' to feel guilty about.

"What do y'all talk about while I'm sleeping?" Tommy asks me after he finally stumbles out of bed. He seemed extra pleased to see me today, even asked me about my day at school.

Tommy lazily smokes a cigarette. "Nothing really." I shrug. "He seems real lonely is all."

"Yeah. Low-down hates it here."

"Why do you call him Low-down?" I ask, stealing the cigarette and taking a shallow puff. I'm not a fan, but I figure I'd better practice. I want to be able to take a drag without coughing and looking lame.

"He didn't tell you?" Tommy asks, taking back the cigarette. He laughs as I sputter up the tiny amount of smoke I inhaled. "Low-down is on the run from the law."

"What?" I ask. "No way."

"It's true... He had to get away so he came down here."

"Tommy, if you're lying to me to make me look stupid..." I slap his arm playfully and he holds up his hands.

"Honest truth, Sweetie. Loew isn't half as good as you think he is."

"I don't really think about him at all," I lie quickly. To show I don't care, I don't ask what Loew even did against the law.

"You're too busy thinking about me, I bet," Tommy whispers in my ear and I giggle. "But you gotta go now. My mom will be home soon."

"Maybe I can meet her sometime," I say, standing up to hunt for my clothes.

"Sure, Sweetie, sometime. I promise."

I dress quickly, over the moon. It's the first time he's said I could meet his mom. I look at him, not wanting to push it. "So I guess I'll see you in school Monday."

He groans. "Why you gotta bring school up?" He throws a pillow at me. "I don't want to go back."

"But you will, won't you?" My voice sounds desperate. "I can't take that place without you."

"Yeah... I'll be there."

I make my way out to the kitchen and head past Loew without so much as a glance in his direction. He gets up to follow me and I hurry outside to my truck.

"Sweetie, is something wrong?" he asks as I slam the door shut.

"Oh, nothing. Just that you failed to mention you was on the run from the law."

His face falls, his mouth hanging open stupidly. "Sweetie, I was going to tell you..."

"It's true?" I ask. I'd hoped Tommy was just teasing me.

"It's not like that. Let me explain."

"Don't worry about it. I should have known you was too good to be true." I thought Loew wanted to be my friend, but what kind of a friend lies like that? Especially when I spilled my guts to him that one day.

My face burns and I feel foolish. I put the car in reverse and back away. Loew stands in the driveway looking devastated, like I was the one that lied to him or something. I drive home, leaving him in my dust. I try to think of how much better school will be with Tommy back, but my mind keeps jumping back to Loew's grief-stricken face.

Tommy would kill me if he knew how much I really care about Loew.

CHAPTER**TWELVE**

When I get home, I jump into the shower right away. I have a late shift at the Dairy Queen. If I time it right, I can get out of the house before Daddy gets good and drunk.

I open the door, letting the steam out around me. The house is really quiet.

When I get to my room, my father sits on my bed. He clutches my phone in his hand. His face is red. At first I think he's drunk. Then I realize he's real angry.

"Daddy?" I ask, my voice cracking.

He looks up at me. "Who's Tommy?"

The blood drains from my body, leaving me cold.

"And why are you texting him such filth?" He throws the phone at me. His aim is off. It flies over my right shoulder and shatters against the wall.

I didn't delete those texts from the other night. Why didn't I delete those texts? I wanted to read them again later. They made me feel special. How could I have been so stupid to leave my phone out?

I should run, but my legs are glued to the floor.

I should say something, but I know it won't make a difference.

He stands and takes off his belt. Fear shoots through my body and settles in a lump in my stomach. I can smell beer on him. He always smells like beer. But he's not drunk. And it's worse when he's sober.

He knows I'm not my mama, but I look so much like her. He can focus all his hatred for her into his arm. He can release it in his blows on my body.

With the first flick of the belt, I collapse against the wall and slump down to the floor. I cover my head and try to make my mind go somewhere else. The pain comes hot and fast. Again and again and again. I cry out.

I'll survive this, though. If there's one thing I know, it's how to take a beating.

CHAPTER**THIRTEEN**

Daddy says I have to quit my job at Dairy Queen. He says I'm only allowed to go to school, then have to come straight back home. He says I'm just like my mother. He calls me stupid trash who should know better. He drinks a little, then. He says some more bad things about my mama. At least the focus is on her instead of me.

Finally, Daddy leaves my room. He tells me to think about what I did. He slams the door behind him. I lay down on my bed, whimpering. The belt marks still burn, but soon they'll just ache. Fade into a dull throb that's easy to take.

I hear my brothers leave their rooms. I hear them talking to Daddy downstairs. Then I hear the sound of the television, loud and comforting.

I lay there and think about what I did, just like Daddy told me to do. But it just makes me think how wrong he is, not how bad I am. So what if I have a little fun with Tommy? I ain't hurting no one.

I think of my brother Matt, who talks about girls like they're not real people. He tells Daddy in great detail how far he got with this girl or that girl. And Jimmy, who Matt is always ragging on for being a virgin. Daddy doesn't tell them to think about what they done.

Anger flares in me. I'd never thought about it before, but Tommy and my daddy are a lot alike. I don't know where things are going with Tommy. If it all worked out, if we became an official couple, we would get married and have kids. I don't want my life to always be like it is right now. I don't want to leave home to make one for myself that's exactly the same. I don't want to ditch out on the family I make.

No, the difference would be me. I would never leave Tommy, like my mama left my daddy. I would never leave my kids like they was nothing to me.

I stand, and let out a groan of pain that flashes across my abdomen. Daddy's always careful about where he hits me. Not on my arms or legs or face. Only on my middle where clothes cover the bruising.

I dress slowly, then shuffle over to my desk and turn on my ancient computer to distract me. I spot Loew's butterfly knife on my desk. I practice opening and closing the blade but the pain is too much. I lay back down on my bed. If I don't move, it don't hurt too bad. I realize I'm still clutching the knife, which brings a smile to my face.

I doze off into blissful oblivion.

CHAPTER**FOURTEEN**

Tommy's not at school Monday.

We're in a lot of the same classes so he must've decided to extend his suspension. I hope he ain't dropping out. He's talked about quitting enough times. Daddy didn't take away my car 'cause I ain't got no other way to get to school. If I hurry, I can see Tommy and head home before Matt can tattle. I'll tell Tommy I'm on lockdown. I'll explain I don't know when I'm going to see him outside of school. He'll have to come back after that.

After school, I drive like I'm fleeing the police. I'm out of the car before I've fully parked. I practically run into his house.

Loew is at the kitchen table. He stands to talk to me. I just shake my head and walk straight to Tommy's room. He's sleeping, so I shake him awake.

"Sweetie, what?" He glares at me. "I'm trying to get

some sleep. Get lost."

"I can't see you no more."

He sits up, looks at me. "What are you talking about?"

"I... my daddy read the texts on my phone and beat me real bad. He says I can't go out anymore. We can see each other at school, though..."

His face tightens and he lets out a small, false laugh. "You're breaking up with me?" He stands and stalks toward me. I back up against the wall.

"Tommy, no..."

He grabs my hair, forcing my face up. "You walk in here, like you have any say over when we end." He pulls hard on my hair.

"Stop it," I whimper, tears starting to flow down my cheeks.

"You and me, we ain't through until I say we're through." He slaps me hard across the face. He releases my hair, letting me fall to the floor. Tommy doesn't have Daddy's rule about not marking up my face or arms. Tommy's rage doesn't have rules.

He takes a step back and I steel myself for the kick I know he's about to take. But it never comes. Instead Tommy is on the floor and Loew is punching him. I stand shakily.

"You coward," Loew screams at Tommy. He hits him again in the face and Tommy's nose spurts blood.

Tommy gets the upper hand though. He could kill Loew with his bare hands, I know. I use all my strength to rip him off of Loew.

Tommy scrambles back and reaches for something under his bed. He finds it and lunges forward, wielding a hunting knife. He comes at me and I think that this is it.

Tommy is really going to kill me.

Loew pushes me out of the way as Tommy slashes, cutting Loew's arm. "This ain't got nothin' to do with you," Tommy tells Loew. "Sweetie is mine."

Tommy rushes me again, pushing past Loew. All the times Tommy hit me and I just let it happen rush through my mind.

I don't want to die.

My hand seems to have a mind of its own as it grabs the knife from my pocket and flicks out the blade. I feel like I'm in a dream. I raise the knife and stab it forward without aim. I even close my eyes.

And then I open them.

CHAPTER**FIFTEEN**

"Sweetie... we have to go. Now."

I look up from Tommy's body and find Loew holding his hand out to me.

"My name is Tessa," I say dumbly.

"Alright, Tessa. We have to leave."

"My mama named me."

Loew steps over Tommy and grabs the knife from my hand, folding it neatly and pocketing it. He grabs me gently by the shoulder and makes me cross the room. "I shouldn't have worn white sneakers," I say.

"Just don't step in the blood," he tells me. I nod numbly.

He leads me to my truck and puts me in the passenger side. Then he drives and drives as I stare out the window.

CHAPTER**SIXTEEN**

It's dark before I talk again.

"When I was a baby, my older brother Matt couldn't say his S's right, so he wouldn't say my name. He just called me T. And my mama said I was such a sweet baby... so my parents started calling me Sweet-T... and now everyone just calls me Sweetie."

"Okay." Loew glances from the road to me.

I look at him. "I want you to know that."

"Sweetie, Tessa... I think we have to have a talk..."

"Tommy's dead, ain't he?" I ask. I know the answer already, but I have to hear it. It doesn't feel like he's dead. It doesn't feel like anything.

"Yes. Tommy's dead."

"And you ain't angry with me?"

"No, of course not. He would've killed you. Then he would've killed me too."

"What now?" I ask. What could we possibly do

now? I begin to sob softly. How do I have any tears left?

"Let's go somewhere we can rest tonight. We'll decide what to do in the morning."

"But Loew, won't they be looking for my truck?"

"I was thinking about that. My aunt didn't know about you, so she can't tell the cops to look for you."

"My dad... I don't know how long before he calls me in as missing. He might think I just ran off for the beating he gave me."

"Then let's get somewhere we can hide this truck."

I nod, uncertain. I continue to stare out the window, tears rolling down my cheeks.

Tommy is dead. And I killed him.

CHAPTER**SEVENTEEN**

That night, we sleep in an abandoned farmhouse.

Loew scouted it out first while I waited down
the road. After a while, he declared it clear. I
park my car in the barn and make my way up the
creaky steps. The people must have just moved out
because it's run-down but not falling down. There's
even an old beater sedan that Loew thinks he can get
working.

I sit on the musty couch and pull an old blanket
around me.

Loew looks through the cabinets and the fridge.
"They left some food. You hungry?" He pulls out a bowl
and some canned soup and pops it in the microwave.

"No. Weird that the electricity is still on," I say.

"Yeah," he grumbles. "We should watch the news."

It's not long before the newsperson starts talking
about me. Well, us.

And now for a hometown tragedy. A local man was brutally attacked and left for dead earlier today. Loew Brewster was staying with his family, on the run from a pending criminal charge in Georgia. Police believe that he murdered his cousin and kidnapped seventeen-year-old Tessa Sheridan. It is unclear her relationship to either Tommy Hicks or Loew Brewster. More details to come in the investigation. The manhunt continues.

They think Loew killed Tommy and ran off with me. A photo of me flashes on the screen. My school picture from last year. Then my daddy is on TV crying. Actually crying. "We just miss our Sweetie so much. That boy needs to be found and punished."

"I knew they'd blame me," Loew says. "You okay, Sweetie?"

I gulp. "Sure. Can we watch something else?"

There's an old black-and-white movie on another channel. I motion for Loew to sit next to me on the couch. He does, but real far away. I wonder if I want him to sit closer or not.

We fall asleep like that, the space empty between us.

CHAPTER**EIGHTEEN**

When I wake up, Loew's arms are around me. My head in his chest. Tommy never held me like that. Loew smells different than him too. Tommy always smelled like cigarette smoke, but Loew kind of smells like rain and the outdoors.

I doze off again, and when I wake, Loew is in the other room. He's showered and changed. He's wearing clothes that look old-timey. Brown pants and a gray shirt. Suspenders. It suits him.

He offers me his hand and I take it. He leads me to the bathroom and turns on the shower for me. He leaves and I find towels and clothes laid out for me. Showering is easy. My body does all the work while my brain remains fuzzy.

I work the soap into a lather and scrub at my skin. After I wash away all the dried blood, I feel much better. Even a little clearer. I dress slowly, slipping on an old yellow sundress. It has that musty smell like everything else in the house, but it seems otherwise clean. It fits really well, as if it were made for me. I braid my wet hair around my head to keep it off my shoulders.

When I step back into the living room, Loew sits on the couch.

"What are we going to do?" I ask.

"I... I've been thinking about it and... I think you can go home."

"What... how?" I sit next to him.

"You can say I did it. They already think I'm guilty. You call the police and say I killed Tommy because I was jealous and you saw the whole thing."

I reach out and touch his arm. He flinches away. "What about you?"

He runs his hands through his dark hair. "Tommy was going to kill me... and no one would care, not really. I mean, my aunt is my dad's stepsister. They don't even have the same last name. I thought it was the perfect place to hide out because no one would look for me there. She only agreed to take me in because I paid her a bunch of cash. Tommy could have killed me, buried the body, and no one would've cared."

"I would've cared," I say quietly.

"Look, I'm sure my aunt already told the cops about me, about what happened in Georgia." Again, I don't ask what he did there. For some reason, it doesn't seem to matter. "If you tell them I killed Tommy, they'll believe you."

I shake my head again. "No, they'll know it was me."

"How?" he asks.

"They have crime scene people. Ain't you ever watched them shows? My DNA is all over that room. They'll know I'm lying."

"What about self-defense?" he says. "Tommy was about to stab you."

I close my eyes and try to remember Tommy's face when he was being sweet. But all I can see is his last moment. I open my eyes and look at Loew. "They might still think we did it on purpose, for revenge. For him always beating on me."

"Then I'll turn myself in. Take the rap. I'm not guilty of that, but I'm not an innocent person."

"I know what we can do," I say quietly.

"What?" He looks at me with wide eyes filled with hope.

I put my hand on his arm again, and this time he doesn't shake me off. "I'll go with you. We'll run together."

CHAPTER**NINETEEN**

"Tessa," he says. My name sounds right coming from his mouth. "If I run, you can't come with me. After what happened in Georgia, just making it down to my aunt's house was hard as heck. Avoiding cops, living each day afraid. And then I had somewhere to go. Now we have nothing. You have to go home. Take your chances."

I stand and face him. Reaching behind me, I unzip my dress and let it fall down around my ankles.

"What are you...?" he gasps as his eyes focus on my stomach. Standing before him in just my underwear, he can see every belt mark, every angry purple welt.

"My dad... he ain't right. Maybe I won't go to jail. Even so, I don't want to go back there." I start to cry softly. "I *can't* go back there."

He nods and kneels at my feet, pulling my dress back up over my battered body. I put my arms through the sleeves.

"Alright, Tessa. If we can get our hands on some money, we have a chance. We can head somewhere far away, up to Canada, maybe."

"I've never been out of Florida," I admit. "Ain't Canada really cold?" A shiver runs through my body.

"Yes, it's cold. We could go through Texas, to South America if you like."

"I don't know Spanish..."

"We'll learn it. It'll be easy."

I smile at him. "Easy," I whisper. My smile turns into a grimace and I break down, sobbing.

For a moment, I forgot. I killed someone. I killed Tommy. I killed the boy I loved. I saved Loew's life. I saved myself. I put my face in my hands, trying to stifle my cries. When am I gonna stop hurting?

Loew reaches over and holds me until I sob myself out.

"Should we stay here a while?" I ask finally.

He shakes his head. "I don't think it's safe. We can take that old car and start heading north to the panhandle. We'll be just another car on the road. But if we stay here, they might search the area and find us."

"So we should go soon..."

"You still want to come with me?" he asks.

"Ain't nothin' happened in the last few minutes to change my mind."

He pulls some keys out of his pocket. "Found these, for that rust bucket outside." He also has a duffle bag he packed. Probably with whatever supplies he could find. "I'll burn our old clothes and then we can go." I see he's already found shoes for me. Some old Mary Janes with a small heel. They fit perfectly as I buckle them into place.

We step through the front door together. The sun hits my skin with gentle heat. Loew takes my hand in his and I smile up at him. I push down my guilt and pain over what I did to Tommy. I push them down to the bottom of the river and use that pain as a stepping stone.

We start a fire in a brick pit. Loew lights some cardboard to get it going. Once it's good and hot, I stand in front of it. The heat of the day and the heat of the fire make me sweat, but it feels good.

One by one, I feed my blood-soaked clothes into the fire. Last are my white sneakers, stained red-brown. I watch them disappear into nothing.

I feel clean.

I feel light.

For the first time in my life, I feel free.

CHAPTER**TWENTY**

We drive for a few hours through back roads. The car AC is broken. We ride with the windows down. The hot air hits me in the face and I feel gritty.

I ask Loew about his life before. He tells me about his deadbeat mom and dad. Their sick relationship that neither of them will quit. He tells me about his friends that he thought of as his real family. Until one by one they moved away, or went to jail, or died.

"I had a best friend. She was a lot like you."

"A girlfriend?" I ask.

"Yeah, a girlfriend." He rubs the stubble on his chin. He looks older than eighteen. "Her family life was real bad. Her stepdad, well, he wasn't a very nice guy. Her mom wasn't much better."

"I seen good parents on TV," I say. "But I think that's the only place they exist."

Loew doesn't laugh. He just says, "Maybe."

"Did they beat her?" I ask.

"That. And other stuff. It got so that she figured she deserved it. It got so that she took all the bad stuff in her life and started to like it. I didn't understand then. I think now that's what she needed to do to get by."

"I... I guess I let Tommy make it so that he was my only friend," I say sadly.

His face tightens. "You know my cousin wasn't exactly a good man."

I'd never thought of Tommy as a man before. He was eighteen, got held back a few grades early on so he was always the oldest in class... but a man? No. Tommy's always been a boy to me. "And you are? A good man?"

He chuckles. "Maybe not good exactly, but I try to take care of the ones I love."

"Like your girlfriend, in Georgia? Did you take care of her? Did you get her away from her parents?"

He takes a deep breath. "Nah. She wouldn't leave. It killed her in the end."

"That's horrible," I say quietly. "Her stepdad...?"

"It was his fault. She got heavy into drugs because of all the things he did to her. She overdosed. She was just treated like another dead junkie."

I don't know what to say, so I don't say anything.

"That's why I'm on the run," he admits. "I don't know what Tommy told you. I shouldn't have gone to confront her stepdad. I was just so angry that he wasn't going to be punished. I went to talk to him and it got out of hand."

"I know the feeling," I say. I don't know if I want to laugh or cry. I don't know if I want to ask what "confront" means to Loew, or just keep myself in the dark about the truth.

CHAPTER**TWENTY-ONE**

At a run-down rest stop in the middle of no-where, we sit in the car and eat crackers from Loew's supply stash. He opens a can of tuna fish that makes the car stink. I pretend to gag until he tosses it out the window. Then we giggle together.

Finally, his face turns grim. "We're low on gas," he tells me. "And we don't have any money."

"What are we going to do?" I ask.

He eyes me. "We might have to... take some gas."

"You mean steal it?"

He nods.

"Like from someone else's car? I seen that on TV."

"No. I mean maybe we could do that. But I was thinking we could... rob a gas station."

I raise my eyebrows. "How we gonna... oh," I say. I understand now.

He looks like he's sorry for what he's saying, but keeps on anyway. "Look, we can scare them up, grab some cash, and be in and out real fast. I bet a lot of these run-down places out here don't even have security cameras."

"But what if someone records us on their phone?" I ask. "The police are already looking for us."

"We'll wait until there's no one around but the clerk. Then we'll handle them. We'll be real careful."

I shake my head. "Maybe we can try it another way."

I expect him to not listen, to want to do it his way. That's what my daddy would do. That's what Tommy would do. Instead he leans back with his head tilted. "What do you have in mind?" he asks.

He listens to my idea. Eventually he nods his agreement. "But I'll still stick around in case you need a backup."

We switch spots so I can drive and I turn the key. I back up out of the rest stop and peel onto the road.

"Woowee," Loew laughs. "Sweetie, girl, I know we're wanted by the law, but maybe don't actually drive it like we stole it!"

CHAPTER**TWENTY-TWO**

We pass a few chain-store gas stations before we find a mom-and-pop one. Loew gets out by the side so it looks like I'm alone. I pull up to the pumps. I check my hair in the rearview mirror. With my Heidi braids and my old-style dress, I look like a church girl. Perfect.

The clerk behind the counter is old. Like, older-than-dirt old. I panic for a bit but then I think that even old guys like to be flirted with. I approach him, making my face worried. It ain't a stretch or nothing.

"What can I do you for, young lady?" he asks with a smile.

I swallow. "Sorry to bug you, sir... I just..." It ain't hard to start crying. I'm only a few seconds from tears at any time anyway.

The old man looks guilty. Like he made me cry. I can work with that.

"Sorry. I just left my purse at home. I'm almost out

of gas."

"Oh, that's too bad. Do you want to use my phone? You can call your folks."

"No. I mean, I would. Obviously. But I can't... my phone was in my purse and I..." For a moment I think I really messed up but the words keep flowing out of my mouth. "I don't have anybody's number memorized. I just look them up in my contacts. You know how it is."

The old man shakes his head. "It's such a shame what technology is doing to this country. A nice young lady like you could get in real trouble. Didn't your mother ever teach you to keep emergency cash in your car?"

"My mother is dead," I tell him. I see it then on his face. I've won.

"It's not your fault, dear. But you really should keep some money and an address book in your glove compartment for times like this."

"Yes, sir. I've learned my lesson."

He nods approvingly.

"I will definitely do that from now on. But if you just give me a little gas, I can be back with money by nightfall," I lie.

"I can let you have twenty, young lady." It couldn't have worked out better. There's no one else around, and he's so old he probably doesn't even know what a smartphone is, much less how to use the camera on one. "What kind of a man would I be to leave a damsel in distress?"

"Thank you," I say, letting the tears dry. Twenty dollars in gas won't get us far, but it's better than nothing. And we didn't have to flash a weapon like we were crazy outlaws or something.

The door chimes behind me and I wonder what Loew is doing. We agreed he would stay out of sight. That way when the guy told on me later, he would say it was only a girl. He might not even report it. Most men don't like to admit that they were conned by someone much younger... and female.

I turn, but it ain't Loew. It's a middle-aged man with a blond crew cut and a huge gut.

He takes me in, sees my wet face, and asks, "You need some help, honey?"

"No. Yes. I just forgot my wallet. I need some gas..." He looks me up and down again, his eyes pausing on my legs, even though I'm wearing a long dress. I shiver 'cause I feel like he can see through my clothes.

"I'll pay for your gas, honey." There's a look in his eyes I don't like. Hunger.

"We figured it out, Jim," the clerk tells him. "This nice young lady... I didn't catch your name, sweetheart."

"Tessa," I say before I can stop myself. Sometimes I am such an idiot.

"Tessa is going to fill up and then swing by later to pay me back."

"No need," the other man—Jim—says. He pulls two twenties out of his wallet. He makes a big show of placing them on the counter. "That should cover her fill-up. Now she owes me instead of you."

I don't like the sound of that. Things are getting messy. "Thank you," I mutter and hurry outside. I quickly grab the gas pump handle and fill up the tank.

I think I got away with it when someone brushes the back of my neck. When I turn, the man from the store—Jim—is behind me. I look over his shoulder. There's no sight of Loew where I dropped him on the side of the building. Jim is looking at me again like he can see through my clothes.

"We didn't talk about how you would pay me back."

I giggle nervously. "If you give me your address..."

"I was born at night, but not last night, honey," he tells me, chuckling at his own joke. "You're not going to come to my house flashing cash."

"So, you're just giving me the money?" But I know he ain't.

The man grabs my shoulder. "Honey, ain't nothing in this world free." He pulls me forward. "You can pay me now." His other hand wraps around my waist and crushes me to his beer belly.

My face is surrounded by his bulk. I can't scream. I

can't even breathe.

But then, there's impact. Loew's fist against the man's head. Over and over. The man is no longer holding me. He's on the ground.

I take a step back. Loew stands next to him, his fist red and tight. His jaw clenched. His eyes dark and mad.

"We gotta go, Sweetie," Loew tells me and pushes me into the car. We drive away, dust flying behind us.

"He was going to hurt you." Loew sounds desperate. "He wanted to hurt you. I couldn't let him," he explains.

Oddly calm, I look at my hands. I don't want to look at Loew. I don't want to believe he has that monster within him. I don't want to believe he can hurt someone so badly with his bare hands. Just like my dad. Just like Tommy.

"Sweetie, I will never let anyone hurt you," Loew tells me. And I believe him.

CHAPTER**TWENTY-THREE**

I don't say anything as we drive out of Florida and into Alabama. I don't say anything when Loew tells me we had to stop for gas one more time. I don't say anything when Loew goes inside. I don't say anything when he comes back out with cash and food and fills the tank. I don't ask how he got those things.

After dark, he pulls the car over in a field and makes a bed for us out of blankets. The night is warm and the sky is filled with stars. I sit next to him on the blanket.

"Do you hate me now?" Loew's voice is small and scared. How can he be so many things at once?

"No," I say, my voice firm.

"I had to hurt that man. If you would've seen the way he was looking at you. I can't let nothing happen to you, Sweetie. Tessa."

"You hurt him bad," I say. "For me."

"I would kill anyone who put a finger on you. I would kill anyone who tried to hurt you." That word *kill* rings in my ears. I convince myself he's being dramatic.

"I been thinking a lot," I tell him. "When you and Tommy was fighting, I had a choice. I thought I loved Tommy, but... I chose you."

I lean over and kiss him. He's surprised at first, but then relaxes. I pull him close. He smells so good. He's so gentle. I thought I loved Tommy, but I ain't never felt like this before in my life. Like Loew and I were two halves of a whole.

We sleep under the stars.

CHAPTER**TWENTY-FOUR**

I know the things we did next was wrong, but there wasn't any other way. It's like a wind was blowing behind us and swept us up along with it. We did whatever we wanted.

If we wanted to eat, we ate. If we wanted to drive, we drove. We bathed in ponds or lakes. We shopped with our stolen money.

When we needed somethin', we took it.

Loew was the perfect gentleman. He did most of the work. I drove the car.

CHAPTER**TWENTY-FIVE**

Things change when we get to Texas.

We stay at a little motel that looks like it's from another time, but we look like we're from another time, so it fits. The lobby needs paint and smells like mold. The clerk takes our cash and doesn't ask any questions. Loew asks him if there's anywhere to get burgers. He offers to let me rest while he goes for food.

I snooze until Loew comes back with our lunch. He brought me a chocolate milkshake that I didn't even have to ask for. I hug him close. I ain't never had no one treat me so kind.

While we eat, I switch on the TV. We watch the news for the first time in two weeks.

Loew and I made the national news.

The Bitter and Sweet Killers are our top story. The couple that started their crime spree in a small Florida town have still not been brought to justice. Armed robberies, as-

sault, and one shooting have left three people dead and many wounded.

I look at Loew. We ain't killed anyone since Tommy and that was self-defense! We don't even have a gun.

Named for Tessa Sheridan, who is known as Sweetie, their first killing was that of her classmate, Tommy Hicks. Their path of destruction led them through several states, where they committed robbery and left countless victims in their path. We can now confirm that Loew Brewster was running from a murder charge in Georgia.

I drop the milkshake on the stained carpet and turn to Loew.

Murder.

But didn't I know that somewhere deep down? Didn't I wonder about the darkness in his eyes, what he was capable of?

"Loew, what have you done?"

Loew looks away. "Everything I've done has been to protect the ones I love."

"Who else have you hurt?" I ask. "Do you have a gun?" I don't really want to know the answer.

The news continues.

The couple was spotted at a Florida gas station, where they assaulted a good Samaritan, Jim Kliner. The gas station clerk told the police that Tessa Sheridan was working with Loew Brewster, not a captive as was previously thought.

Loew stands and turns off the TV. "You don't have

to watch that."

"Then tell me the truth," I demand.

"I should've roughed up that old man at that first gas station so he didn't talk. I did take care of the next gas station attendant in the panhandle. And I had to take care of a clerk in Alabama," he tells me. "And... things got out of hand at a jewelry store in Louisiana."

Take care of? What did that even mean? Hurting is how you take care of someone?

"You robbed a jewelry store... I thought we were just taking what we needed. Is that when I woke and found you gone that one day?" I thought he'd left me alone in the swamp. I'd never been so sad in my life.

Loew nods. He pulls something out of his pocket. It's a ring box. He kneels before me.

"This ain't exactly how I wanted to do this," he tells me. "But... you know I love you, Sweetie."

I stare down at him. He looks so hopeful and I feel my heart jump in my chest. I love him, I do, but I'm also horrified at what he's done. I reach out for the diamond ring in the box. Before I can take it, there's a crash behind us.

The motel door explodes inward.

CHAPTER**TWENTY-SIX**

Loew tackles me and we fly over the bed. We crouch behind it as the room fills with smoke.

"Cops," Loew says with a cough. "They found us. I knew a motel was risky."

He pulls a handgun from under the bed. There it was. Did he have it all this time? When I let him go into stores and gas stations to *take care of things*?

He begins firing. His shots are wild, but a police officer collapses nearby.

Loew shoots at the doorway while pulling me into the bathroom.

"They'll have the room surrounded, but we have to try to get out," he says as he pushes me toward the window.

I fall out onto the concrete and scrape my knees and hands. He follows and someone to our left shouts:

"Stop!"

Shots are fired between us. Loew then pushes me along to the tree line behind the motel.

"I had to do it," Loew tells me as we run. He's grabbing my arm, hard. It feels like all the other times hands have bruised my skin. I know then how strong he is. I know then what he's capable of. I'm done pretending I don't.

I think about Tommy. About the blood on my shoes.

It was self-defense then. It wasn't a choice.

But I will never hurt anyone again.

CHAPTER**TWENTY-SEVEN**

We get about a mile before I notice something is wrong with Loew. He's slowing down and clutching his side. He turns to me, his face white.

"Sweetie, I didn't want you to worry and slow us down but... they shot me."

"We gotta keep going, Loew." I rip some of the fabric off the skirt of my dress and wrap it around his belly. "They ain't gonna stop coming for us."

I half-carry him. I don't know how bad Loew is hurt. His blood comes out a bright red and leaves wet dots on the ground.

Eventually we have to stop. Loew can't go on anymore. I lay him on the ground.

We lost all of our supplies. All of our money. He's shaking and I hold him tightly. A dog barks in the distance. My head jerks up.

"We gotta find that river we drove over to get to the

motel. If we cross it, we'll be less easy to track," Loew says.

"Can you make it that far?"

He stands up, his face pale. He might be dying. What would my life be without him? Even after all he did, he's all I've got.

"Still got that ring?" I ask.

He groans and digs in his pocket and pulls it out. I can see his wide grin in the low moonlight. I hold up my hand and he places it on my finger. I hold it out and watch it sparkle.

"I love you, Tessa," he tells me.

I begin to cry. "I love you too, Loew. These last few weeks have been the best of my life."

I look up into his eyes and bring my mouth to his. I kiss him like I'm dying and his love is the only thing that can save me.

I hear a dog bark—closer now.

"They're coming," Loew tells me. I hear other noises. The cops are on our trail.

He rushes now, determined. I barely have to help him at all. Maybe he's not shot as bad as I feared. Maybe he'll be just fine.

We find the river by accident. It's more of a stream. We splash into it at a run. I hope it will still work to wash away our scent. Loew leads the way, right down the middle of the water. He's jogging now and I really think we'll be okay. We're both soaked through and the going is hard. My shoes catch on stones and my calves ache, but I keep up with him.

We make it another mile or so before Loew collapses. He falls face-first into the water. I panic and grab his arm and swing him around so he doesn't drown. Red plumes around him.

"Can't go much further," he tells me, sputtering. "Drag me to the shore and we can make a stand."

"I don't want to kill no one else," I tell him. My tears run off my cheeks and join the flow of water in the stream.

"You got to," he says, his voice surprisingly strong. "It's them or us. I'd kill them all to protect you." He coughs up blood. "This ain't the end of us." He sounds like Tommy and for an instant I'm afraid of him.

"Let's just turn ourselves in. Get you help."

"They ain't gonna help me. They'll lock us up and we'll never see each other again. I'd rather go out fighting." His lips are stained red.

Love swells in my chest and I almost agree. Go out in a blaze of glory. But I know that's not right. Those cops are just doing their jobs. They don't deserve to get hurt. Neither did those gas station clerks. Or even Tommy. People are more than just bodies.

"What if we get away with this?" I ask. "What then?"

He smiles. "We'll start again. We can make it to Mexico."

A stick breaks on the stream bank and my head jerks up. I expect to see the cops on top of us. Instead, it's a kid with a fishing pole. He can't be more than eight years old. He looks like Jimmy when Jimmy was still just a sweet little boy. His mouth opens in a wide O.

Loew takes out his gun and I act before I can think. I scramble on top of him for it. I ain't gonna let him kill a little kid. Even shot, Loew is still stronger than me and I have to use all my weight to hold him down.

I'm on top of him, my knee in his chest before his grip loosens. Finally, I wrestle the gun from him. The kid is long gone, run off into the woods.

And then Loew's head is under the water. His blank eyes stare up at me.

"Loew?" I ask, shaking him.

I'm sobbing now. "Loew, I love you." I tell him.

I lied to myself when I promised I wouldn't kill no one else. Because of me, Loew is dead.

I lift him up and hold him in my arms.

It's a long while before I let go. Loew drifts peacefully down the river.

I watch after him until he's gone.

AFTER

I finish my soda and crush the can. The woman with the kind eyes—my proxy guardian—has tears streaming down her face. Even the cop stares at me with a sympathetic look.

"After that, I turned myself in."

The cop turns off the recording device and gives me a hard look. "You're under stress. I don't think you understand the consequences of pleading guilty..."

"Yes," my proxy jumps in. "You were forced..."

"Weren't you listening? Ain't nobody forced me. I may have been stupid, but I committed crimes too."

"Your story might make a judge be lenient. I could talk to the prosecutor—"

"Look, lady," I tell her. "I killed the boy I loved... probably the only person in the whole world who really loved me back. Lock me up. Throw away the key." I cross my arms, determined. "I deserve what

I get."

The female cop gets up to go, then turns back to me. "But why? If you were happy? Loew was hurt and bleeding. Why did you choose some random kid over him?"

I could have had a life with Loew. One where we hurt everyone we came in contact with just to save each other. We could have blamed poverty, blamed our parents, blamed those who hurt us first.

"I've had a lot of people beat me down," I tell her. "I've had so much pain. I couldn't become someone who made other people hurt. I couldn't let Loew keep on doing what he done."

She nods her understanding, then leaves.

I don't know what will happen to me.

No matter what happens, I knew some kind of love. For once in my life. Which is more than I thought I'd ever have.

No matter what happens, for a little while, I knew love.

But in the end, I chose what love meant.

WANT TO KEEP READING?

If you liked this book, check out another book
from West 44 Books:

AND THE MOON FOLLOWS
BY CYN BERMUDEZ

ISBN: 9781538385296

CHAPTER ONE

Mornings at my house are always buzzing with activity, especially on the first day of school. The earthy scent of coffee wakes me and I check the time. Ten minutes before my alarm. I turn it off and pull the covers over my head. I want to fall back to sleep, but I hear feet shuffling busily, socks on wood. Next, I hear the thump of shoes. I remove the covers from my face and open my eyes. Light filters into my room, creating lines of shadow as the light seeps through the blinds.

My younger brother and sister are awake. They always seem to be in unison. They have been since birth, being twins and all. They move about the house together fussing over everything—shoes, hair, clothes. Their outfits usually match. I hear them at the table, pouring cereal, spoons clanking. Right now, they're excited about the first day of school. I wish I could say the same.

Finally, I stumble out of bed. My morning ritual is the same, school or not. I head straight for the kitchen and pour myself a glass of orange juice. The cold, tangy juice helps me start my day. The twins are already at the table.

Mom bought the twins matching khaki pants and white polo shirts. My sister, Sophie, has a pretty pink headband over her short hair. Mike's hair is short on the sides. The top is gelled into a wave. Their hair is the only difference between the two. They're fraternal twins, but their face structure is almost identical.

As for me, the first day of school is overrated. And it's not because I don't like school. I actually *like* learning. I'm just not interested in the "who's got more" dance. My wavy, almost-straight hair hangs over my shoulder. My bangs, which I trimmed last night, are slightly skewed. I have my outfit laid out on my bed–my favorite vintage *Goonies* t-shirt with a hole in the lower right corner, and of course, my favorite jeans, the ones I've had since the seventh grade. I've sewn them several times. Multi-colored threads are stitched awkwardly down the thigh area, where my pants always rip. I aim for comfort over pizzazz.

"Morning, brats," I say.

The twins are on their phones playing a game. Sophie and Mike look up at me.

"Good morning," they say.

Mike returns to his game but Sophie stares at me for a bit. I wonder what she's thinking.

"What?" I ask. I assume she's checking out my clothes. My little sister is... *fashion sensitive.* She takes after our mom in that way. Worries about hair, clothes, and shoes—too much if you ask me. Hope, my best friend, is similar, so I'm used to it. I clarify, "This is *not* what I'm wearing to school."

I'm wearing pajamas! Still, I feel I have to state the obvious.

"Can you blame me for wondering?" Sophie says.

She's so snarky for a nine-year-old.

A horn honks outside. The twins begin to rush. One last spoonful. Their spoons ding against the bowls. Their uneaten cereal begins to turn to mush. Leaving early in the morning is normal for them. The twins play sports with the same groups of kids. Last year, the parents took turns giving rides to school. The same for this new school year. The twins gulp the rest of their juice. Their plastic cups are on the table at the same time. Their chairs scrape across the kitchen floor. I feel a gust of wind as they run for the door.

My phone chimes. Hope texted me her outfit. Brand new dark-colored jeans. An off-white peasant shirt. Short-sleeved with puffy shoulders.

Hope sends me another text, "Please tell me you're not wearing those god-awful jeans!"

I text her back, "@@." Rolling my eyes emoji.

Just then my stepdad, Frank, walks into the kitchen.

"Always on that phone, Luna," he says.

He heads straight for the coffee. His hair is slicked back with the same gel Mike uses.

"No, I'm not," I say.

He doesn't look at me. Instead, he fixes himself a cup of coffee. The coffee is set on a timer. Mom prepares it before she leaves to work at night. If my mom doesn't pre-make the coffee, it doesn't get made. At least not by Frank. I'd have to do it. And if not me, Sophie would have to make coffee if he wanted it bad enough.

"You set the example for your sister and brother," he says.

It bugs me that he thinks he knows what's best. He entered our lives permanently a couple of years ago. What does he know? Nothing.

"Why do they even have phones?" I ask. I seriously get blamed for everything around here.

"Don't sass me, girl," Frank says. His Okie accent is strong despite his efforts to sound "Hollywood," as he puts it.

He gulps down the rest of his coffee. When he finishes, he sets his cup down on the counter. I place my glass in the sink and head back to my room.

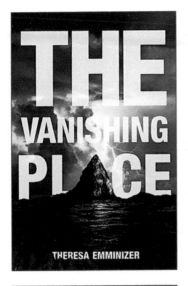

THE VANISHING PLACE

THERESA EMMINIZER

The Water Year

Max Howard

ON THE PLUS SIDE

P.A. KURCH

AND THE MOON FOLLOWS

CYN BERMUDEZ

CHECK OUT MORE BOOKS AT:
www.west44books.com

An imprint of Enslow Publishing

WEST **44** BOOKS™

ABOUT THE AUTHOR

Demitria Lunetta is the author of the YA books **THE FADE**, **BAD BLOOD**, and the sci-fi duology, **IN THE AFTER** and **IN THE END**. She is also an editor and contributing author for the YA anthology, **AMONG THE SHADOWS: 13 STORIES OF DARKNESS & LIGHT** and **BETTY BITES BACK: HORROR STORIES FOR YOUNG FEMINISTS**. Find her at demitrialunetta.blogspot. com, on Twitter @DemitriaLunetta, and on Facebook at facebook/DemitriaLunettaAuthor.